This Book Belongs To:

Bright

Sparks

Thank you for buying this Bright Sparks book.

We donate one book to less fortunate children for every two sold.
We have already donated over 150,000 books.

We want to help the world to read.

This is a Bright Sparks book
This edition published in 2002
Bright Sparks, Queen Street House,
4 Queen Street, BATH BA1 1HE, UK
Copyright © Parragon 2001

this book was created by
small world creations ltd

Printed in China.
ISBN 1-84250-525-4

Fred the Fearless Fireman

Bright ☆ Sparks

Fred the Fireman hurried to the fire station. It was his turn to cook lunch, and he had just bought some nice, plump sausages at the butcher's.

At the fire station, Fred bumped into Builder Benny, who had come to repair a broken window frame.

"Ooops! Hello, Benny!" he said.

Then he went straight to the kitchen to start cooking.

The smell of *sausages* wafted through the fire station.

"**Mmm**, those sausages smell good!" said Dan and Mike,
the other firemen, as they arrived for work.

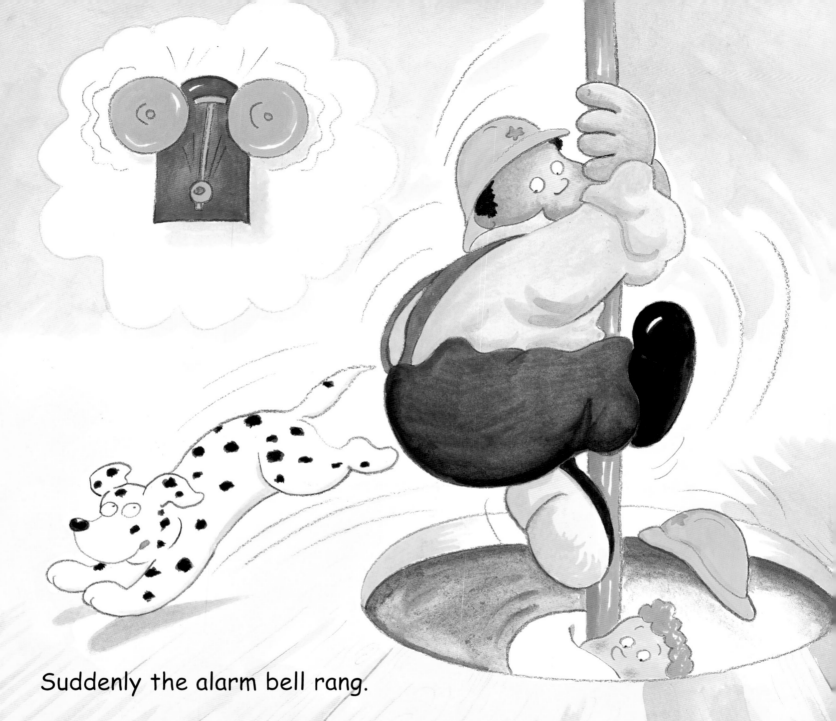

Suddenly the alarm bell rang.

CLANG! CLANG! CLANG!

"Emergency!" cried Fireman Mike. He and Fireman Dan
rushed down the pole and into their fire-fighting gear.

The emergency was in Tony's Pizza Parlour.
One of the ovens had caught fire! Fred rushed in with
a big fire extinguisher. Dan and Mike followed with the hose.

With a WHISH! and a WHOOSH! from Fred,
and a SPLISH! and a SPLOOSH! from Mike and Dan,
the fire was soon out.

Tony's
Pizza
Parlour

Just when they were ready to go back to the station, the firemen heard a call coming through over their radio.

"Emergency! Emergency! Window cleaner in distress on Pine Avenue. Emergency! Over."

"We're on our way!" said Fireman Fred, starting the engine.

NEE-NAW! NEE-NAW!

With sirens blaring, the fire engine zoomed onto Pine Avenue. Some people had gathered in front of Number 26.
"It's Vet Vicky's house!" said Fred.

"It's Will the window cleaner!" cried Postlady Polly. "He always cleans Vet Vicky's windows while she's at work. But today his ladder fell down and broke, and now he's stuck. His leg is hurt too, can you help him?"

"Certainly!" said Fireman Fred. "I'll be up there in a jiffy!"

The firemen put up their ladder, and Fred fearlessly scrambled up.

"Here I come, Will!"
he shouted.

"I've got you, Will!" said Fred. As everyone cheered, Fred carried Will down the ladder and helped him into the fire engine.

Fred drove the fire engine straight to the hospital.
"Thank you for rescuing me," Will said to Fred.

"Don't mention it," said Fred. "I'm sure your leg will be fine,
but I think you'll need a new ladder!"

"What a busy day it's been!"
said Fireman Fred, as they drove
back to the fire station.
"Our work's not over yet!"
said Fireman Dan.
"Look! There's smoke up ahead!"

NEE-NAW! NEE-NAW!
went the siren as they raced to the scene of the fire.

The smoke was coming from the fire station! Dan and Mike unwound the hose, and Fred raced inside. "Oof!" he gasped, as he tripped over the hose and bumped into Benny again!

"Sorry, fellows," said a red-faced Builder Benny.
"I burnt the sausages. I think your lunch is ruined."

Suddenly Fred had an idea.

"Tony!" said Fireman Fred.
"His pizzas are yummy, and an extra-large one
will be a perfect lunch for all of us!"